SHAPES AROUND ME

Squares

Anita Loughrey

What is a square?

This is a *square*. A *square* has four *sides* that are the same and four corners.

Follow your finger around the edge of the square.

Who lives in the house with the *square* windows?

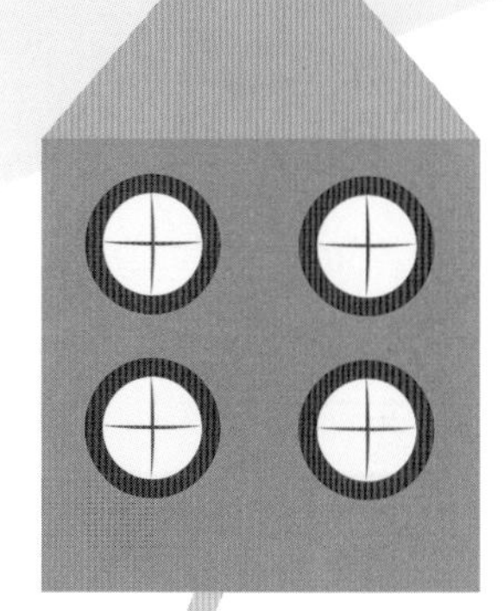

Suki

Joe

Rebecca

Counting squares

Point to the *squares* in the pictures.

Answer: 8 squares

How many *squares* are there on the *back* of the lorry?

Look out of the window. Can you see any square shapes on cars or lorries?

Answer: 4 squares

Big and small

Squares can be
different sizes.

big

bigger

small

smaller

Look around your house. Can you find a big square shape?

biggest

smallest

Coloured squares

Squares can be different colours.

How many blue squares can you see?

How many green squares can you see?

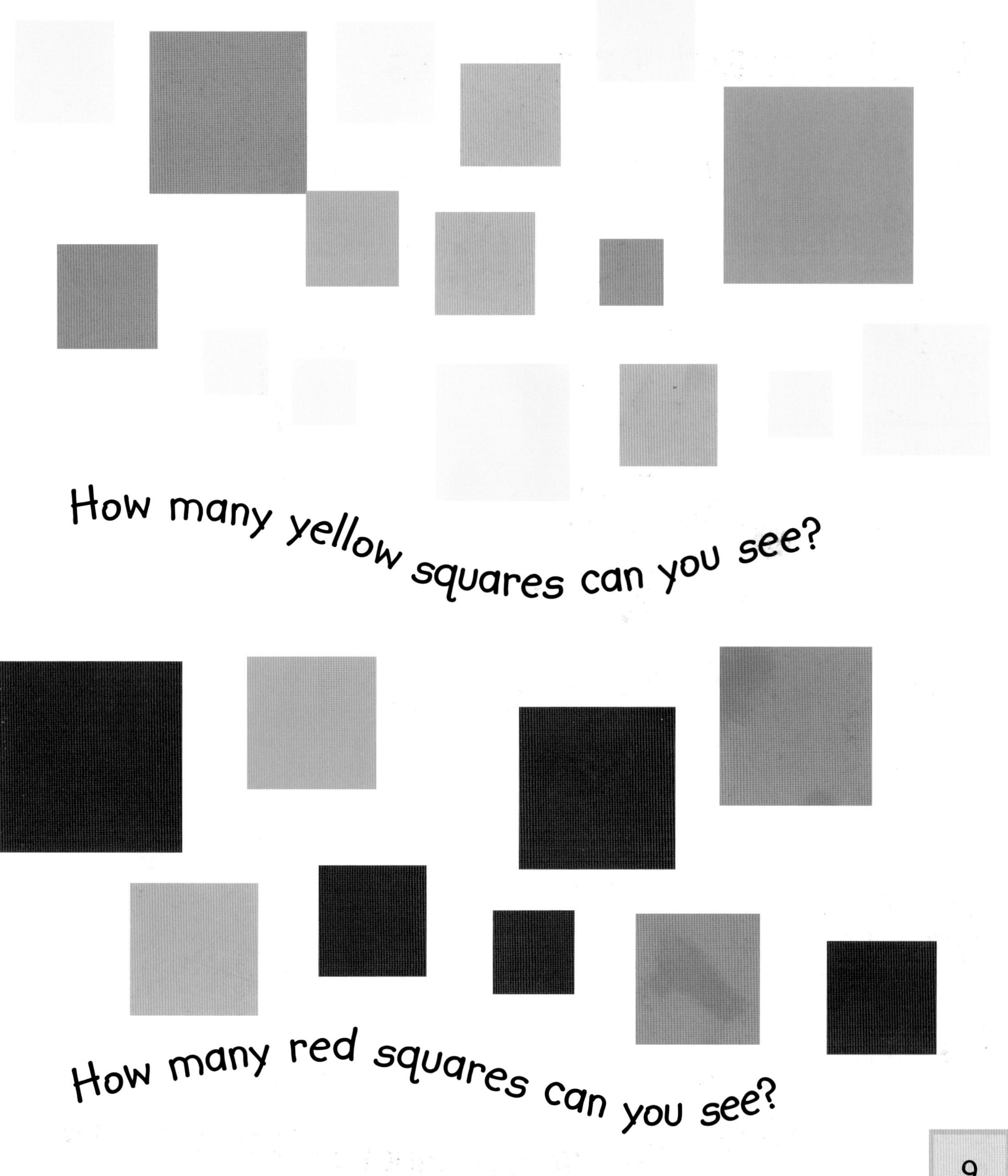

How many yellow squares can you see?

How many red squares can you see?

Answers: 2 blue squares, 4 green squares, 8 yellow squares, 5 red squares

Let's go shopping!

Help the car follow the path to get to the market stall.

Look out of the window. Point to any square shapes you can see.

How many *squares* does the car pass?

Answer: 8 squares

Drawing squares

Ask an adult to help you to draw this house.

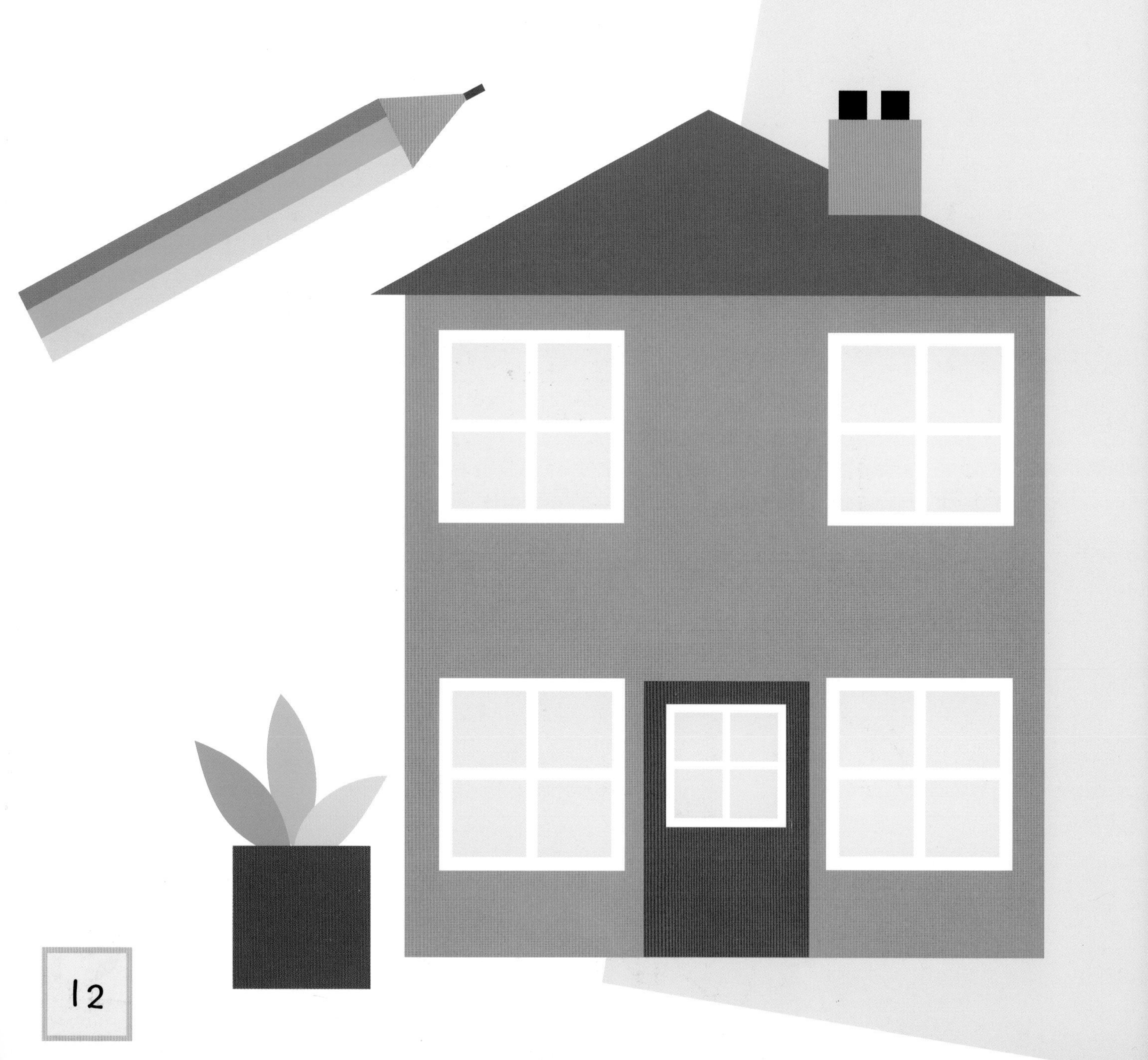

Ask an adult to help you to draw this present.

Happy Birthday

In the town

Point to the squares in the picture. Can you spot them all?

window

shopping bag

phone

flower tub

Can you see any of these square shapes when you go out?
Gorgeous Gifts
dustbin
camera
drain

In the living room

Point to the squares in the picture. Which squares are small?

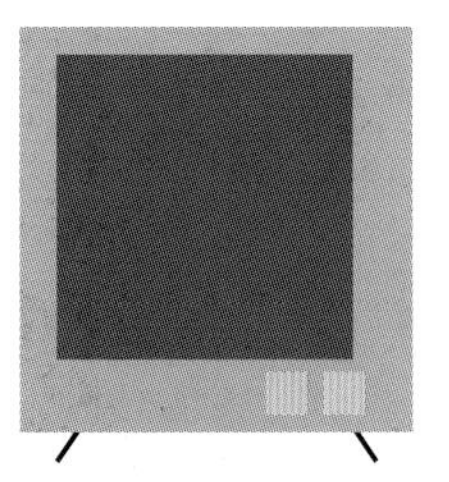

TV

light switch

fireplace

picture

What square shapes can you see in your living room?
lamp
cushion
vase

In the restaurant

Point to the *squares* in this picture. Can you find more than five *squares*?

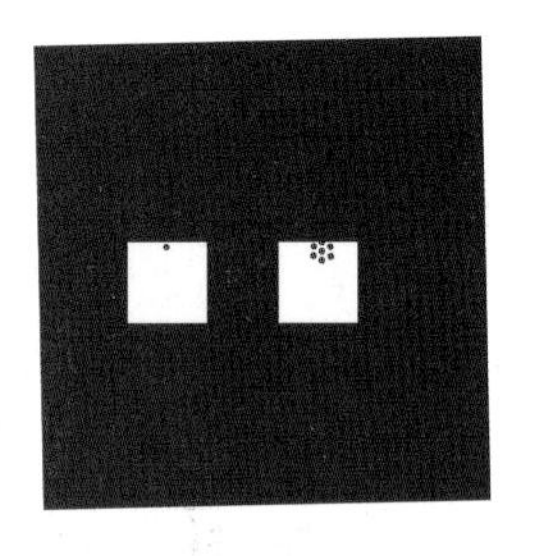

table

till

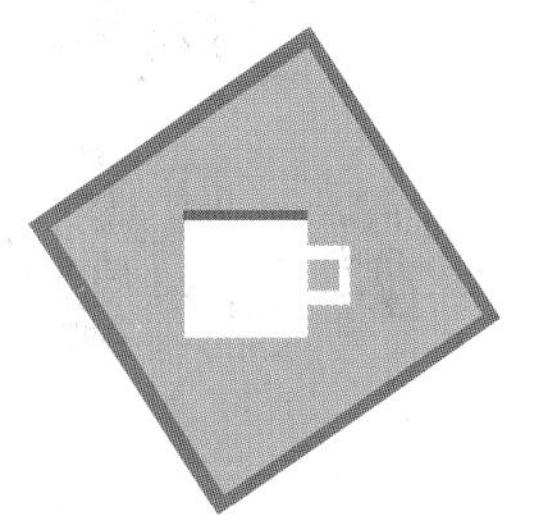

tray

coffee machine

Are tables always square? What other shapes can they be?
notepad
clock
lampshade

In school

Point to the *squares* in the picture. Are there more than eight *squares*?

jigsaw

paintbox

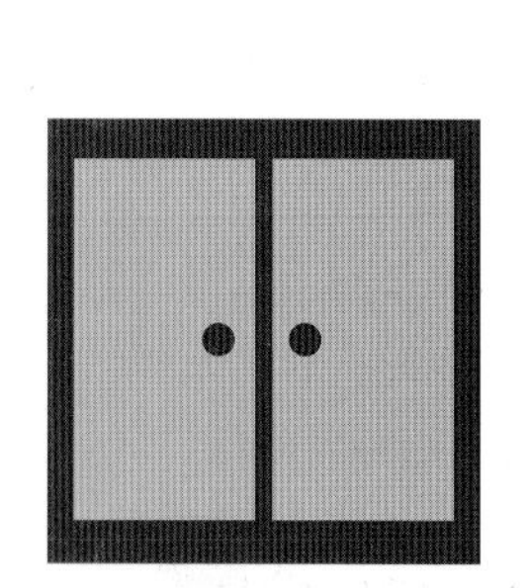

cupboard

computer

What squares can you see in your classroom?
notice board
picture
toybox

At the castle

Point to all the *squares* in the picture. How many can you *see*?

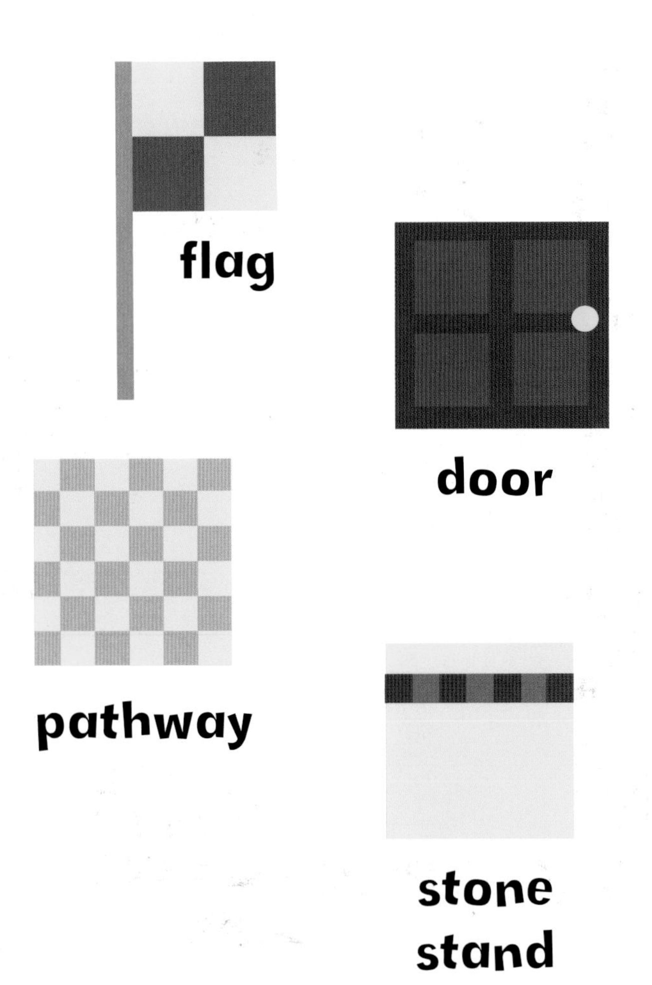

Look out of the window. Can you see any square shapes on buildings?
shield
flower bed
gate

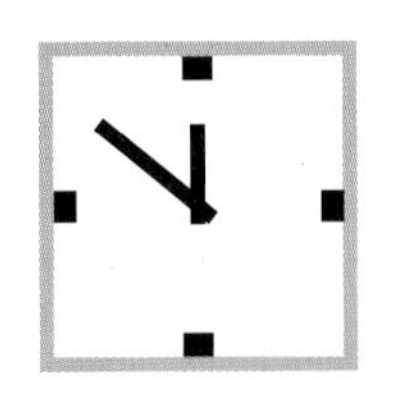

Notes for parents and teachers

This book has been designed to help your child recognize squares and to distinguish them from other shapes. The emphasis is on making learning fun, so the book uses the environment to reinforce what your child has seen in the book. The activities help your child to understand the idea of a square shape by using familiar, everyday objects.

Sit with your child and read each page to them. Allow time for your child to think about the activity. Encourage them to talk about what they see. Praise your child when they recognize the items shown in the book from their own experience. If any of the items are unfamiliar to your child, talk about them and explain what they are and where they might be found. Whenever possible, provide opportunities for your child to see the items in the everyday world around them.

Other activities for you to try with your child are:

* Play games such as, 'I spy with my little eye something square shaped that begins with...'.
* Cut out pictures of different-shaped objects from a catalogue and ask your child to sort them by shape, or to match them to pictures in this book.
* Encourage your child to look for things that are square shaped when you are out and about, or play this game at home.
* Let your child make collages or junk-models of different square objects, or mould them in clay, so that they can explore the shape by touch.

Remember to keep it fun. Stop before your child gets tired or loses interest, and try again another day. Children learn best when they are relaxed and enjoying themselves. It is best to help them to experience new concepts in small steps, rather than to do too much at once.

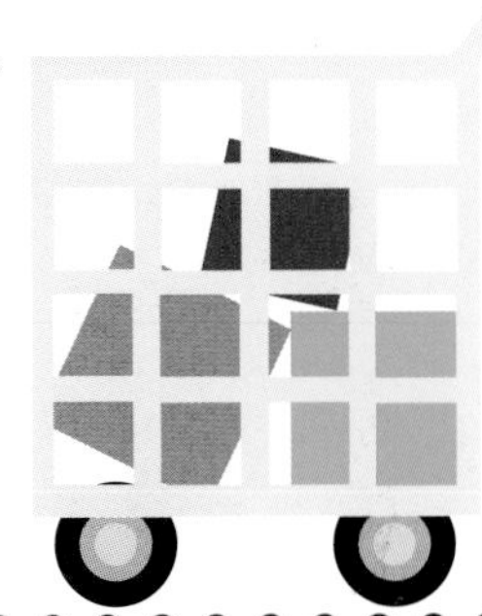

Illustrator: Sue Hendra
Editor: Amanda Askew
Designer: Susi Martin

Educational consultant:
Jillian Harker

First published in the UK in 2010 by
QED Publishing
A Quarto Group company
226 City Road
London EC1V 2TT

www.qed-publishing.co.uk

A catalogue record for this book is available from the British Library.

ISBN 978 1 84835 473 9
Printed in China